MW01121828

YOU'RE ALL MINE

For Owen ...
Life has challenges and rewards. You are my reward.
XOXO Mommy

Thank You to:

My Family
Dale Lockley
Victory Reproductive Centre
Windsor Regional Cancer Centre
RMA of Michigan
4 SV Glenwood Public School

ISBN: Softcover 978-1-5434-6377-4
EBook 978-1-5434-6376-7

Print information available on the last page

Rev. date: 11/30/2017

To order additional copies of this book, contact:
Xlibris
1-888-795-4274
www.Xlibris.com
Orders@Xlibris.com

I think you’re super.

I think you’re sweet.

I think you’re special.

I think you’re neat.

And you’re ALL MINE!

When shopping at the grocery store,

You wave and smile at people coming through the door.

I think you're super.

I think you're sweet.

I think you're friendly.

I think you're neat.

And you're ALL MINE!

When eating meals and snack time too,

You enjoy each bite even when it’s something new.

I think you’re super.

I think you’re sweet.

I think you’re hungry.

I think you’re neat.

And you’re ALL MINE!

When stacking blocks and rings up high,

Your wheels are spinning, asking “how and why.”

I think you’re super.

I think you’re sweet.

I think you’re curious.

I think you’re neat.

And you’re ALL MINE!

When trying to find your favourite book,

You won't read one because it's more fun to look.

I think you're super.

I think you're sweet.

I think you're learning.

I think you're neat.

And you're ALL MINE!

PUZZLES

When climbing furniture you ought not to,

Using all your muscles to make your dreams come true.

I think you're super.

I think you're sweet.

I think you're strong.

I think you're neat.

And you're ALL MINE!

When you run too quick then fall and crash,

After cuddles you're off again in a flash.

I think you're super.

I think you're sweet.

I think you're tough.

I think you're neat.

And you're ALL MINE!

When in the tub you splash and play,

Blowing bubbles and cooing in your own cheerful way.

I think you're super.

I think you're sweet.

I think you're silly.

I think you're neat.

And you're ALL MINE!

When you rub your eyes and tug your ear,

And want to snuggle oh so near.

I think you're super.

I think you're sweet.

I think you're sleepy.

I think you're neat.

And you're ALL MINE!

When your bottle is done and I've tucked you in,

Already excited for the next day to begin.

I think you're super.

I think you're sweet.

I think you're incredible.

I think you're neat.

And you're ALL MINE!

No matter the adventures and challenges ahead,
know you'll do your best because you're ALL MINE!

Printed in the United States
By Bookmasters